To my sons, Trevonn and Tayden

Brother: A Grief Story

Text © 2013 by Teleah Scott-Williams
Illustrations © 2013 by Somnath Chatterjee
ISBN: 978-0-9888398-4-7 (Print Version)
ISBN: 978-0-9888398-5-4 (Kindle Version)
Library of Congress Control Number: 2013911342

Printed in the United States of America

A Message to Parents, Teachers, Caregivers, and Other Adults
As an adult, you know the heartbreak caused by the death of a loved one. Since death is permanent and sometimes misunderstood; children especially, need to be supported throughout the grieving process. Acknowledging to a child that their grief is real is important. Giving them coping strategies to deal with the loss of a loved one is beneficial and reassuring that they will be okay.

BROTHER

A GRIEF STORY

TELEAH SCOTT-WILLIAMS

ILLUSTRATIONS BY SOMNATH CHATTERJEE

My name is Jackson.
My brother died and I am very sad.

I live with my Mom, Dad, and my sister, Jasmine.

I am the youngest. This is our story about grief and how we are learning to heal as a family.

At first, I cried a lot because I missed brother. I had no one to play ball or video games with anymore.

When I was sad, Jasmine would give me a great big hug
and she would tell me that everything would be okay.

Mom and Dad would hug me too.

They would also hug Jasmine when she was feeling blue.

I like hugs because they make you
feel all warm and fuzzy on the inside.
Hugs are great to give and receive.

Sometimes it's hard to talk about brother dying. When I can't talk about my feelings, Mom tells me to write a few minutes in my journal.

I have pictures in my journal. Many of the pictures are of brother and me. Sometimes, I just like to look at the pictures. They make me happy because they remind me of the good times we spent with brother.

What I miss most about brother is his smile.

He wore braces on his teeth for two years and when the dentist removed his braces, brother had the most perfect teeth I had ever seen. Brother was always telling jokes and making me laugh. I think brother's new teeth helped him to be funny.

We laugh a lot lately. Mom, Dad, Jasmine, and I sit around the table after dinner and we talk about the good times we had with brother. We all miss brother.

Sometimes, I laugh until my stomach hurts. Jasmine laughs so hard that she almost falls out of her chair.

We know brother would want us to be happy. So, we keep on laughing and sharing our favorite memories.

I am happy that Dad allowed me to
keep some of brother's things.

I have brother's football helmet, his basketball, his high school jersey, and his lucky pair of socks with a hole in one big toe.

I keep brother's things safely stored in a box in my room. Every now and then, I like to look through the box and try some of the things on.

I can't fit in any of brother's things because
I still have a lot of growing to do, but I make
sure that I take good care of his things.

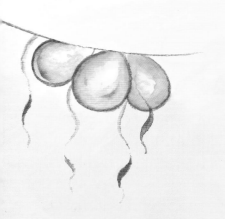

Mom, Dad, Jasmine, and I plan to light a candle for brother on his birthday every year. We will sing his favorite song and eat his favorite cake and ice cream. This was my idea.

Dad says brother lives in a special place called heaven. Mom says brother is a heavenly angel. Jasmine says I should feel very special to have an angel watching over me.

One day, I hope to grow up to be just like brother. He was the best big brother anyone could have. Every night before I go to bed, I pray to God that he would give brother special wings.

It's my way of saying thank you to a brother who means so much to me.

Teleah Scott-Williams' life has been a courageous journey of tragedy and triumph. The unexpected death of her son, Timothy, sparked her to conduct research to deepen her understanding and knowledge about sudden cardiac death in young athletes. In doing so, she gleaned a deeper insight on how important it is for young athletes to receive early heart screenings. A native of Harrisburg, Pennsylvania, Teleah currently resides in Owings Mills, Maryland, with her family. *Brother* is her first children's book on grief and loss. Her other title, *Free To Grieve: A Mother's Memoir In Black and White* is available online through Amazon and Barnes & Noble.